HORRiD HENRY
and the
Mummy's Curse

HORRiD HENRY
and the
Mummy's Curse

Francesca Simon
Illustrated by Tony Ross

Orion
Children's Books

Horrid Henry and the Mummy's Curse originally appeared in
the black and white storybook of the same title
first published by Orion Children's Books in 2000
This edition first published in Great Britain in 2015
by Orion Children's Books
an imprint of Hachette Children's Group
a division of Hodder and Stoughton Ltd
Carmelite House
50 Victoria Embankment
London EC4Y 0DZ
An Hachette UK Company

1 3 5 7 9 10 8 6 4 2

The paper and board used in this paperback are natural
ecyclable products made from wood grown in sustainable forests.
The manufacturing processes conform to the environmental
regulations of the country of origin.

A catalogue record for this book is available from the British Library.

ISBN 978 1 4440 1527 0

Printed in China

www.orionchildrensbooks.com
www.horridhenry.co.uk

*For Joshua, Daniel and Libby
who live in Gibraltar
near the Rock of Gibraltar*

There are many more
Horrid Henry Early Reader books available.

For a complete list visit:
www.horridhenry.co.uk
or
www.orionchildrensbooks.com

Contents

Chapter 1

Tiptoc.

Tiptoe.

Tiptoe.

Horrid Henry crept down the hall.
The coast was clear. Mum and Dad
were in the garden, and Peter was
playing at Tidy Ted's.

Tee hee, thought Henry,
then darted into Perfect Peter's room
and shut the door.

There it was. Sitting unopened on
Peter's shelf. The grossest, yuckiest,
most stomach-curdling kit
Henry had ever seen.

A brand-new, deluxe "Curse of the Mummy" kit, complete with a plastic body to mummify, mummy-wrapping gauze, curse book, amulets and, best of all, removable mummy organs to put in a canopic jar.

Peter had won it at the
"Meet a Real Mummy" exhibition
at the museum, but he'd never even
played with it once.

Of course, Henry wasn't allowed into
Peter's bedroom without permission.
He was also not allowed to play
with Peter's toys.

It was so unfair,
Henry could hardly believe it.

True, he wouldn't let Peter touch
his Boom-Boom Basher, his Goo-
Shooter, or his Dungeon Drink kit.
In fact, since Henry refused to share
any of his toys with Peter, Mum had
forbidden Henry to play with any of
Peter's toys – or else.

Henry didn't care – Perfect Peter
had boring baby toys – until, that is,
he brought home the mummy kit.

Henry had ached to play with it.
And now was his chance.

Chapter 2

Horrid Henry tore off the wrapping,
and opened the box.

WOW! So gross!
Henry felt a delicious shiver.
He loved mummies.

What could be more thrilling than looking at an ancient, wrapped–up DEAD body? Even a pretend one was wonderful. And now he had hours of fun ahead of him.

Pitter-patter!

Pitter-patter!

Pitter-patter!

Oh help, someone was coming
up the stairs!

Horrid Henry shoved the mummy kit
behind him as Peter's bedroom door
swung open and Perfect Peter
strolled in.

"Out of my way, worm!"
shouted Henry.
Perfect Peter slunk off.
Then he stopped.

26

"Wait a minute," he said.
"You're in my room! You can't order
me out of my own room!"

"Oh yeah?" blustered Henry.

"Yeah!" said Peter.

"You're supposed to be at Ted's,"
said Henry, trying to distract him.

"He got sick," said Peter.

He stepped closer.
"And you're playing with my kit.
You're not allowed to play with any
of my things. Mum said so.
I'm going to tell her right now!"

Uh oh. If Peter told on him
Henry would be in big trouble.

Very big trouble.

Chapter 3

Henry had to save himself, fast.

He had two choices.
He could leap on Peter
and throttle him.
Or he could use weasel words.

"I wasn't playing with it,"
said Henry smoothly.
"I was trying to protect you."

"No you weren't," said Peter.
"I'm telling."

"I was, too," said Henry.
"I was trying to protect you from the
Mummy's Curse."

Perfect Peter headed for the door.
Then he stopped.

"What curse?" said Peter.

"The curse which turns people into mummies!" said Henry desperately.

"There's no such thing," said Peter.

"Wanna bet?" said Henry.

"Everyone knows about the mummy's curse. They take on the shape of someone familiar but really, they're mummies. They could be your cat – "

"Fluffy?" said Peter.
"Fluffy, a mummy?"

Henry looked at fat Fluffy snoring
peacefully on a cushion.

"Even Fluffy," said Henry.

"Or Dad.

Or Me.

Or you."

"I'm not a mummy," said Peter.

"Or even – "
Henry paused melodramatically
and then whispered, "Mum."

"Mum, a mummy?" gasped Peter.

"Yup," said Henry.

"But don't worry. You help me
draw some Eyes of Horus.
They'll protect us against… her."

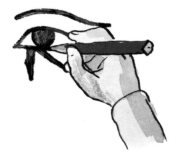

Chapter 4

"She's not a mummy," said Peter.

"That's what she wants us to think,"
whispered Henry.

"It's all here in the Mummy curse
book." He waved the book
in front of Peter.

"Don't you think the mummy on the
cover resembles you-know-who?"

"No," said Peter.

"Watch," said Henry.
He grabbed a pencil.

"Don't draw on a book!"

Henry ignored him and
drew glasses on the mummy.
"How about now?" he asked.

Peter stared. Was it his imagination or
did the mummy look a little familiar?

"I don't believe you," said Peter.
"I'm going straight down to ask
Mum."

"But that's the worst thing you
could do!" shouted Henry.

"I don't care," said Peter.
Down he went.

Henry was sunk. Mum would probably cancel his birthday party when Peter blabbed.

And he'd never even had a chance to play with the mummy kit.

It was so unfair.

Chapter 5

Mum was reading on the sofa.

"Mum," said Peter,
"Henry says you're a mummy."

Mum looked puzzled.
"Of course I'm a mummy," she said.

"What?" said Peter.

"I'm your mummy," said Mum,
with a smile.

Peter took a step back.
"I don't want you to be a mummy,"
said Peter.

"But I am one," said Mum.
"Now come and give me a hug.

"No!" said Peter.

"Let me wrap my arms around you,"
said Mum.

"NO WRAPPING!" squealed Peter.
"I want my mummy!"

"But I'm your mummy," said Mum.

"I know!" squeaked Peter.
"Keep away, you… Mummy!"

Perfect Peter staggered up the stairs
to Henry.

"It's true," he gasped.
"She said she was a mummy."

"She did?" said Henry.

"Yes," said Peter.
"What are we going to do?"

Chapter 6

"Don't worry, Peter," said Henry.
"We can free her from the curse."

"How?" breathed Peter.

Horrid Henry pretended to consult
the curse book.

"First we must sacrifice to the
Egyptian gods Osiris and Hroth,"
said Henry.

"Sacrifice?" said Peter.

"They like cat guts, and stuff like that," said Henry.

"No!" squealed Peter. "Not… Fluffy!"

"However," said Henry, leafing through the curse book, "marbles are also acceptable as an offering."

Perfect Peter ran to his toybox and scooped up a handful of marbles.

"Now fetch me some loo roll,"
added Henry.

"Loo roll?" said Peter.

"Do not question the priest
of Anubis!" shrieked Henry.

Perfect Peter fetched the loo roll.

"We must wrap Fluffy in the
sacred bandages," said Henry.
"He will be our messenger between
this world and the next."

"Meoww," said Fluffy,
as he was wrapped from
head to tail in loo paper.

"Now you," said Henry.

"Me?" squeaked Peter.

"Yes," said Henry, "Do you want to free Mum from the mummy's curse?"

Peter nodded.

"Then you must stand still and be quiet for thirty minutes," said Henry. That should give him plenty of time to have a go with the mummy kit.

Chapter 7

Henry started wrapping Peter.

Round and round and round went the loo roll until Peter was tightly trussed from head to toe.

Henry stepped back to admire his work. Goodness, he was a brilliant mummy-maker!

Maybe that's what he should be when he grew up.

Henry, the Mummy-Maker.

Henry, Mummy-Maker to the Stars.

Yes, it certainly had a ring to it.

"You're a fine-looking mummy,
Peter," said Henry.
"I'm sure you'll be made very
welcome in the next world."

"Huuunh?" said Peter.

"Silence!" ordered Henry.
"Don't move. Now I must utter
the sacred spell...

"By the powers of Horus,
Morus, Borus and Stegosaurus,"
intoned Henry, making up all the
Egyptian-sounding names he could.

"Stegosaurus?" mumbled Peter.

"Whatever!" snapped Henry.

"I call on the scarab! I call on Isis!
Free Fluffy from the mummy's curse.
Free Peter from the mummy's curse.
Free Mum from the mummy's curse.
Free – "

"What on earth is going on in here?"
shrieked Mum, bursting through
the door.

"You horrid boy! What have you done to Peter? And what have you done to poor Fluffy?"

"Meoww," yowled Fluffy.

"Mummy!" squealed Peter.

Chapter 8

Eowww, gross! thought
Horrid Henry, opening up the
plastic mummy body and placing
the organs in the canopic jar.

The bad news was that Henry had been banned from watching TV for a week. The good news was that Perfect Peter had said he never wanted to see that horrible mummy kit again.

What are you going to read next?

Have more adventures with
Horrid Henry,

or save the day with Anthony Ant!

Become a
superhero with Monstar,

float off to
sea with
Algy,

or have your very own Pirates' Picnic.

Grow carrots with

Lottie and Dottie,

make magic with The Witch Dog,

and cast a spell with

The Three Little Magicians.

Enjoy all the Early Readers.